HORRID HENRY'S BEDTIME

Francesca Simon spent her childhood on the beach in California, and then went to Yale and Oxford Universities to study medieval history and literature. She now lives in London with her English husband and their son. When she is not writing books she is doing theatre and restaurant reviews or chasing after her Tibetan Spaniel, Shanti

HORRID HENRY'S BEDTIME

Francesca Simon

Illustrated by Tony Ross

Dolphin Paperbacks

First published in Great Britain in 2005
by Dolphin Paperbacks
a division of the Orion Publishing Group Ltd
Orion House
5 Upper Saint Martin's Lane
London WC2H 9EA

The text of *Don't be Horrid, Henry* was originally
published as a picture book with colour illustrations
by Kevin McAleenan

ISBN 1 84255 142 6

A catalogue record for this book
is available from the British Library.

Our grateful thanks to Paper Management Services Ltd
Paper Manufactured by Storaenso Publication Paper

Printed in Great Britain by
Clays Ltd, St Ives plc

www.orionbooks.co.uk

CONTENTS

HORRID HENRY'S BEDTIME

'What are you doing in my room?' screamed Horrid Henry.

How dare Peter come into his bedroom? Couldn't he read the sign?

SMELLY TOAD BROTHERS KEEP OUT

'Looking for my blue pencil,' said Peter. He stared at the piles of comics and sweet wrappers and dirty clothes and toys littering the floor, the bed and the chest of drawers.

'Well it's not in here, so get out,' hissed Henry. So what if he'd pinched Peter's pencil? He'd had a huge bit of sky to colour in. 'And don't you dare touch anything.'

'You should be in your pyjamas,' said Perfect Peter. '*I* am.'

'Whoopee for you,' said Horrid Henry. 'Now get lost.'

Peter wrinkled his nose. 'Your room stinks.'

'That's 'cause you're in it, smelly.'

'Mum!' screamed Peter. 'Henry called me smelly.'

'Stop being horrid, Henry!' screamed Mum.

'Smelly, smelly, smelly,' jeered Henry. 'Smelly, smelly, smelly.'

'MUM!' wailed Peter. 'He did it again.'

'Tattle-tale!'

'Meanie!'

'Poo breath!'

'Stinky!'

'Mega-stink!'

2

Perfect Peter paused. He'd run out of bad names to call Henry.

Horrid Henry had not run out of bad names to call Peter.

'Baby! Nappy-Face! Ugg! Worm! Toad! Ugly! Pongy-Pants! Duke of Poop!'

'MUUUUMMMMM!' screamed Peter.

Mum and Dad burst into the room.

'That's enough!' shouted Mum. She looked at her watch. 'It's eight o'clock. Why aren't you in your pyjamas, Henry? Bedtime, both of you.'

'Hurray,' said Perfect Peter. 'I love going to bed.'

What? Bedtime?

The hateful, horrible word thudded round the room.

'NO!' shrieked Horrid Henry. It couldn't be bedtime *already*.

'I'm sorry I've been naughty, Mum,' said Perfect Peter. 'I was so busy doing tomorrow night's homework I didn't notice the time.'

'Don't worry,' said Mum, smiling.

Then she scowled at Henry.

'Why aren't you ready for bed? Peter is.'

'I'm not tired!' screamed Henry. 'I don't want to go to bed.'

'I do,' said Perfect Peter.

Mum sighed.

Dad sighed.

'Henry, you know the rules,' said Dad. 'In bed at eight. Lights out at eight-thirty.'

'It's not fair!' screamed Henry. 'No one goes to bed at eight.' Except for Lazy Linda, who was asleep at seven, no one went

to bed so early. Toby went to bed at nine.
Margaret went to bed at nine-thirty (so she
said, though Henry wasn't sure he believed
her). Ralph didn't even have a bedtime.

But no. His mean, horrible parents hated
him so much they shoved him into bed
when everyone else was still rampaging
and having fun.

Bedtime. Bleeech. What a hateful, horrible,
evil word. A word, thought Horrid Henry
bitterly, as horrid as *cabbage*, *prison*, *Peter*,
and *school*. When he was King any parent
who dared to tell their
kids to go to bed would
be sent to bed them-
selves at five o'clock
forever.

AAARRGGHH! Why did he have to go to bed? He had TV to watch! Computer games to play! Comics to read!

'But I'm not tired!' howled Henry.

'We're growing boys, Henry, and we need our rest,' said Perfect Peter. 'Early to bed, early to rise, makes a boy healthy, wealthy—'

'Shut up, Peter,' snarled Henry, pouncing.

He was Hurricane Henry, blowing away the last remaining human.

'AIEEEEEEE!' screeched Peter.

'Stop being horrid, Henry!' yelled Mum.

'Go to bed this minute!' yelled Dad.

'NO!' shouted Henry.

'Yes!' shouted Mum.

His parents didn't have a bedtime. Oh no. They could stay up as late as they liked. It was so unfair.

'I'm not tired and I won't go to bed!' shrieked Henry. He lay on the floor, kicking and screaming.

Mum looked at Dad.

Dad looked at Mum.

'My turn to put Peter to bed,' shouted Dad, trying to be heard over Henry's howls.

'*My* turn to put Peter to bed,' shouted Mum. 'I got Henry into bed last night.'

'Uhh uhh . . . are you sure?' screeched Dad. He looked pale.

'YES!' shouted Mum. 'How could I forget? Come on, Peter, what do you want for your bedtime story?'

'*Sammy the Snuggly Snail*,' said Perfect Peter, scampering off to bed. '*Slimy the Slug* was too scary.'

Mum scampered after him.

'I WON'T GO TO BED! I want to

watch *Cannibal Cook!*' howled Henry.

Cannibal Cook was this
brilliant new
TV show
where chefs
competed
to see who
could cook
the most
revolting
meals. Last

time *Gourmet Greg* had whipped up lizard
eyes in custard.
Tonight
Nibbling Nigel
was fighting
back with
jellied worm
soufflé.

'It's so *boring*
being in bed,'
screamed Henry.

'I don't care,' said Dad firmly. 'It's bedtime – now!'

Strange, thought Horrid Henry as he paused for breath between shrieks. At night, he never wanted to get into bed, but in the morning he never wanted to get out of it.

But now was not the time for philosophy. He had important work to do if he was going to delay the evil moment as long as he possibly could.

'Just let me finish my drawing.'

'No,' said Dad.

'Please.'

'N-o spells no,' said Dad.

'It's my homework,' lied Henry.

'Oh all right,' said Dad. 'Hurry up.'

Henry drew a dragon very slowly.

Dad looked at the clock. It was 8:35.

'Come on, Henry,' said Dad. He stood there tapping his foot.

Henry coloured in the dragon very very slowly.

'Henry . . .' said Dad.

Henry drew the dragon's cave very very very slowly.

'That's enough, Henry,' said Dad. 'Now

brush your teeth and get into bed.'

'I've already brushed my teeth,' said Henry.

'Henry . . .' said Dad.

'Oh all right,' said Horrid Henry. After all, he held the record for the world's slowest tooth brusher.

Slowly Henry brushed his front teeth. Slowly Henry brushed his back teeth.

Brush.

Brush.

Brush.

Brush.

Brush.

Dad stood in the doorway glaring.

'Hurry up!'

'But Dad,' said Horrid Henry indignantly. 'Do you want me to get fillings?'

'Bed. Now.'

'You'll be sorry when my teeth all fall out because you stopped me from brushing them,' said Henry.

Dad sighed. He'd been sighing a lot lately.

Horrid Henry stood at the bottom of the stairs.

'I can't walk – I'm too floppy,' said Horrid Henry.

'So crawl,' said Dad.

'My legs are too wobbly,' moaned Horrid Henry.

'So wobble,' said Dad.

Delicious smells floated up from the kitchen. Mum was cooking spaghetti with meatballs. Only his favourite dinner. How could he be expected to go to bed with all that good cooking going on downstairs?

'I'm hungry,' said Henry.

'The kitchen is closed,' said Dad.

'I'm thirsty,' said Henry.

'I'll bring you water once you're in bed.'

Dad was being tough tonight, thought Horrid Henry. But not too tough for me.

11

And then suddenly Horrid Henry had an idea. A brilliant, spectacular idea. True, his parents could make him go to bed – eventually. But they couldn't make him *stay* there, could they?

Horrid Henry yawned loudly.

'I guess I am quite tired, Dad,' said Horrid Henry. 'Will you tuck me in?'

'I said, get into – what did you say?'

'I'm ready for bed now,' said Henry.

Horrid Henry walked upstairs to his bedroom.

Horrid Henry got into his pyjamas and jumped into bed.

'Goodnight Dad,' said Henry.

'Goodnight Henry,' said Dad, tucking him in. 'Sleep well,' he added, leaving the room with a big, beaming smile on his face.

Horrid Henry leapt out of bed. Quickly he gathered up some blankets and a pile of dirty clothes from the floor. Then he stuffed blanket and clothes under the duvet. Perfect, thought Horrid Henry. Anyone glancing in would think he was snuggled

up in bed fast asleep under the covers.

Tee hee, thought Horrid Henry.

He tiptoed to the door.

The coast was clear. His parents were safely in the kitchen eating dinner, leaving Henry a whole house to have fun in.

Sneak

    Sneak

        Sneak

Then suddenly Henry heard his parents' voices. Yikes! They were coming upstairs.

Henry darted back into his bedroom and hid behind the door.

'He's in *bed*?' said Mum incredulously. 'Before nine o'clock?'

'Yup,' said Dad.

'This I have to see,' said Mum.

His parents stood outside his bedroom peeking in.

'See?' whispered Dad proudly. 'I told you, you just have to be firm.'

Mum marched over to Henry's bed and pulled back the duvet.

'Oh,' said Dad.

Horrid Henry slipped out of his room and dashed downstairs. There was only one thing to do. Hide!

'HENRY!' bellowed Dad, running down the hall. 'Where are you? Get back in bed this minute!'

Horrid Henry squeezed under the sitting room sofa. They couldn't make him go back to bed if they couldn't *find* him, could they?

'Have you found Henry yet?' he heard Dad call Mum.

'No,' said Mum.

Tee hee, thought Horrid Henry.

'Is he in the loo?' said Mum.

'No,' said Dad.

'The kitchen?'

'No,' said Dad.

'Maybe he's gone to bed,' said Mum. She sounded doubtful.

'Fat chance,' said Dad.

Henry heard Mum and Dad's footsteps coming into the sitting room. He held his breath.

'Henry . . .' said Dad. 'We know you're in here. Come out this minute or you're in big trouble.'

Henry kept as still as he could.

Mum checked behind the sofa.

Dad checked behind the TV.

Hmmn.

'I'll check Peter's room,' said Mum.

'I'll check Henry's room again,' said Dad.

The moment they left the room, Henry leapt out and dashed to the coat cupboard in the hall. They'd never find him here.

Henry made himself comfy and cosy in the corner with the wellies. Ahh, this was the life! He'd be safe here for hours. Days. Weeks. When the coast was clear he'd sneak out for food and comics. No more school. No more bed. He'd never leave his little hidey hole until he was grown up and could stay up forever.

Uh oh. Footsteps.

Henry jumped up and dangled from the coat rail, hiding himself as best he could behind the coats.

Dad flung open the cupboard door.

Horrid Henry hung on to the coat rail. His feet dangled.

Please don't find me, thought Henry. Please, please don't find me.

Dad pawed through the coats.

Horrid Henry held his breath.

He hung on tighter and tighter . . .

Dad closed the door.

Phew, thought Henry. That was close.

CR—ACK!

CRASH!

Coats, rail and Henry collapsed to the floor.

'Hi Dad,' said Horrid Henry. 'What are you doing here?'

All was not lost, thought Horrid Henry as he lay in his boring bed with the lights off. His mean, horrible parents could make him go to bed, but they couldn't make him sleep, could they? Ha ha ha. He'd been *pretending* to be asleep. Now that the coast was clear – party!

Henry took his torch, a big stash of comic books, sweets, toys, his cassette player and a few Driller Cannibal tapes

and made a secret den under his duvet.

Now, this was more like it.

'Tear down the school! Don't be a fool!'
warbled the Driller Cannibals. 'Watcha
waitin' for?'

'Ahh, don't be a fool!' sang Henry, stuff-
ing his face with sweets.

'What's going on in here?' screamed
Dad, flinging back the duvet.

Rats, thought Henry.

Dad confiscated his flashlight, food,
comics and tapes.

'It's eleven o'clock,' said Dad through gritted teeth. 'Go to sleep.'

Horrid Henry lay quietly for thirty seconds.

'I can't sleep!' shouted Henry.

'Try!' screamed Mum.

'I can't,' said Henry.

'Think lovely thoughts,' said Dad.

Horrid Henry thought about monsters.

Horrid Henry thought about ghosts.

Horrid Henry thought about burglars.

Horrid Henry thought about injections . . .

'DAD!'

'What?'

'The hall light isn't on.'

Dad plodded up the stairs and turned it on.

'Dad!'

'WHAT?'

'My door's not open enough.'

Dad trudged up the stairs and opened it.

'Dad!'

'What?' whimpered Dad.

'Where's Mr Kill? You know I can't sleep without Mr Kill.'

Dad staggered up the stairs.

'I'll look for him,' said Dad, yawning.

'And I need to be tucked in again,' said
Henry.

Dad left the room.

Horrid Henry was outraged. Humph,
wasn't that just like a parent? They nag and
nag you to go to bed and when you tell
them you're ready to sleep, suddenly they
don't want to know.

Henry waited. And waited. And waited.

21

The clock said 11:42.

Still no Dad. And no Mr Kill.

'Dad?'

There was no answer.

'Dad!' hissed Henry.

Still there was no answer.

Henry jumped out of bed. Where was Dad? He needed to be tucked in. How could they expect him to sleep without being tucked in?

Henry peeped into the hall.

No Dad.

Henry checked the bathroom.

No Dad.

He walked downstairs and checked the kitchen.

Still no Dad.

What a rotten father, thought Horrid Henry. To abandon his son without tucking him in . . .

Henry peeked into the sitting room.

'Dad?'

Dad was lying on the sofa holding Mr Kill and snoring.

'Hey Dad, wake up!' shrieked Horrid Henry. 'I'm ready for bed now!'

DON'T BE HORRID, HENRY

Henry's life was perfect.
Then Peter arrived.
This is how it all began.

Henry was a horrid baby.

He screamed in the morning, he screamed in the evening. At night he never slept.

He put breakfast on his head, lunch on the floor, dinner on the walls. And his nappies . . . what a stink!

Then Peter was born.

Peter was a perfect baby. He smiled all day and slept all night. His nappies were never dirty (well, almost never).

Henry was not very happy when Peter arrived. In fact, he was furious.

'I've had just about enough of this baby,' he said to Mum.

'Gootchie gootchie goo,' said Mum.

'Time to take that baby back to the

hospital,' he said to Dad.

'Who's my little plumpikins?' said Dad.

Henry glared at Peter. This house isn't big enough for both of us, he thought.

Horrid Henry tried posting Peter. He tried dumping Peter. He tried losing Peter. He tried letting the wind blow him away.

Perhaps he'll leave, thought Horrid Henry hopefully.

Unfortunately, Peter didn't. He just grew bigger and bigger, sitting in Henry's chair, playing with Henry's toys, swinging on

Henry's swing, and being a total nuisance.

'Mum! Peter's kicking me!' screamed Henry.

'Don't be a tell-tale, Henry!'

'Dad! Peter's bashing Mr Kill!'

'He's only little, Henry!'

'Dad! Henry's knocking down my Lego!'

'Don't be horrid, Henry!'

'Why doesn't Peter ever get into trouble?' muttered Henry.

Then Henry had a wonderful, wicked idea.

'Peter,' said Henry sweetly, 'would you like to dig a hole to China?'

'Oh yes,' said Peter.

Henry pointed to Mum's newly dug flowerbed.

'Dig here,' he said. 'It's easier.'

Peter started digging. Soon there was a lovely big hole.

'That's great work, Peter,' said Henry. 'Why not show Mum?'

Peter toddled off.

Tee hee, thought Henry.

Mum came outside.

'AARGGHHH!' she screamed. 'Henry! How dare you dig up my flowerbed!'

'I didn't do it,' said Henry. 'Peter did.'

'Don't be horrid, Henry!' shouted Mum. 'Go to your room!'

'It's not fair!' wailed Henry.

Next day, he tried again.

'Let's surprise Mum and draw her a beautiful picture,' said Henry. 'How about a Viking ship?'

'Yeah!' said Peter.

'We need a huge space,' said Henry. 'I know! Let's draw on the wall.'

'On the wall!' said Peter.

'We just couldn't fit a whole Viking ship on a tiny piece of paper,' said Henry. 'And just think how pleased Mum will be when she sees it.'

'Okay,' said Peter.

Henry giggled and sneaked off. This time *he'd* get Mum himself.

'Mum, Mum, Peter's doing something terrible!' said Horrid Henry. 'He's drawing on the walls!'

Mum ran upstairs.

'I didn't do it, my hand did,' said Peter. 'It was Henry's idea.'

'No it wasn't!'

'Don't be horrid, Henry!' shouted Mum.

'But I didn't do anything!' said Henry.

'You're the eldest! You should have stopped him,' said Mum. 'Go to your room!'

The next day Mum took Henry and Peter to the park. Henry felt very sad. He couldn't get rid of Peter, and he couldn't get Peter into trouble. Maybe he could push Peter into a puddle when Mum wasn't looking.

Suddenly a huge dog ran up to Peter.

'GRRRRRRRR!' snarled the dog.

'Help!' squeaked Peter.

Henry didn't stop to think. 'GO AWAY DOG!' he howled in his most horrid voice.

Peter started screaming.

Mum ran up. 'Don't be horrid, Henry!' she shouted.

'Henry's not horrid,' said Peter. 'He saved me.'

'My hero!' said Mum.

Henry allowed his mother to hug and kiss him. He supposed he was happy to be a hero for a day.

But tomorrow – *watch out!*

HORRID
HENRY'S
DIARY

Miss Battle-Axe said everyone had to keep a
diary for a day. What a dumb, boring
assignment! Why can't homework ever be
playing computer games, or watching TV?
But no. I have to write about a day in my
life. I already know how I spend my time!
This is cruelty to children and I'm not
writing a single word. I've got far too much
else to do. So there. You can't make me.
Ha ha ha.

Who cares if Mum and Dad find out I
haven't done my homework and ban me from
the computer for a month and take away my
pocket money and unplug the TV and say
no more crisps . . .

Oh all right. I'll write it.

But *never* again.

~~8:00~~ 8:00. am
The alarm goes off. I ignore it.
No way am I going to ~~sho~~ school.

8:05
The alarm goes off again.
I ignore it.

8:06
Mum yells at me to get up.
I hide under the doovay

8:07
Dad yells at me to get up
I pretend it's a bad dream.

8:12
Peter comes in and says I'll
be late for ~~sh~~ school if I
don't get up. **G__oo__d** I say.

~~Nacher Nater Natt~~
Naturally, he's alreddy dressed.

<u>8:14</u>
Mum pulls the koovay off and
screams at me to get up and
get dressed **NOW.**

I say I feel
sick and I
can't go to school. Mum
doesn't believe me.

<u>8:15</u>
I heeve my heavy bones out of bed.
I think makeing children
get up at the crack off dawn
to go to school is cruel and
unusual punishment

<u>8:16</u>
I find some clothes under
the bed and put them on.
I can't find any socks that
match

← my
socks

So I grab some from the
dirty clothes basket

<u>8:20</u>

I go downstairs. Peter is
alreddy eating breakfast.
He likes moosli. I like
Scrummy Yummies.
Mum yells at me for wearing
a dirty T-shirt. Dad yells
at me for not pulling my
chair closer to the table.
But hoo cares if some of
my brekfast gets all over my
clothes and the floor? I don't.

<u>8.40</u>

Yikes! I can't find my schod bag.

8:44

I find my schoolbag. What is it doing under the sofa?

8:45

Uh oh... I can't find my PE kit

8:48

I still can't find my PE Kit. Mum yells at me for not finding it.

8:49

I can't ~~do my~~ find my homework because I didn't do it. Oh well. Maybe Miss Battle-Axe will forget to ask us to hand it in.

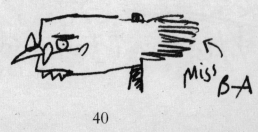

Miss B-A

8:50

We leeve the house to walk to school. Dad asks me if I've brushed my teeth. Yes I say

8:51

I come back home to brush my teeth. We set out again.

8:53

Emergensy! I've forgotten my packed lunch. We rush back to get it.

8:55

Dad, Peter and I run like mad and get to school just as the final bell is ringing at 9:05

<u>9:05 — 3:30</u>

<u>School</u>. Work, work, work, work, work. Ugh. My best subject is lunch. I am briliant at: eating, trading carrots for choclat and food fights. After lunch we do more work. I get into trouble for pokeing William, tripping Linda, shoving Dave, pinching Andrew, copying Clare, making rude noises, chewing gum, not doing my homework and talking in class. That's not so bad. In fact, that's prakticaly a perfect day. I bet I get mentioned in the Good as Gold Book!

~~3:00~~

School Ends. Yippee!

4:00

I stretch out in the comfy black chair with a bag of crisps and switch on Rapper Zapper. **Bliss**.

4:12

Peter says it's his turn to watch Daffy and her Dancing Daisies It's not fair!

4.22

Ralph phones. We make plans for tomorrow

4:45

I'm sent to my room for snatching the clicker and changing the channel to Mutant Max.

4:45 — 6:00
I read comic books.

6:01
Dad, yells at me to come down
and lay the table. I don't
here him. Well, I was busy.

6:10
I come downstairs very
slowly and am to late too
set the table. Boo hoo.

6:15 — 7:00
Dinner. I hate peas, so I
flick them at Peter, and
kick him. When he's not
looking I snatch some of
his chips HMMM, boy,
do those chips tast great!

x

Mum tells me of for chewing
with my mouth open.

Dad tells me off for not using
my fork.

Mum tells me of for spitting

Dad tells me of for making a mess

Mum tells me of for calling
Peter an ugly toad and a
smelly nappy

They both tell me of for flicking
peas at Peter and for kicking
him. But I'm happy because Peter
didn't notice I snatched his chips
                    Tee hee.

7:10 — 8:00

I screem and yell that I won't have a bath.

8:00 — 8:02

I have a bath

8:03

I tell Mum I don't have any homework. This may not be entirely true. But if I have homework I didn't write down what it was, and anyway I lost the worksheet Miss Battle-Axe may have handed out and there's no point in calling Ralph because he won't know about any homework so reely I don't have any homework

8:04 — 8:15

I dance around my room
singing along with the Driller
Cannibals. I turn up the
music as loud as I can.
Mum and Dad screem at me
to make it softer. I don't
hear them - how could I ?
My music was loud! They burst
into my room and turn of
my tape. They are the meanest,
Most horrible parents in the
world and I hate them.

Mum

Dad

8:16 — 8:25

I go into Peters room, and grab some
of his toys. Then I sneek back
into my room.

<u>8:30</u>

Peter says I've taken some
of his toys. I tell him I
haven't. Peter tells Mum.
I get into trouble. BUT I
will be revenged!

<u>8.30 — 9:00</u>

I red a fantastic book about
a great kid who is always
getting into trouble and who
has a horrible younger brother
who's perfect and two super
mean parents. I can't
remember the title but
I reely recomend it.

9:00

Lights out. Time for my trusty flashlight to continue reading under the covers.

9:32

Mum confiscates my flashlight. Just as well I have another one!

oops again

2:23 am

Yawn. Goodnight

JUST WONDERING

Everything you've
always wanted to
know about Horrid
Henry. Francesca
Simon tells all!

How did you get the idea for Horrid Henry?

I got the idea for Horrid Henry when a
friend asked me to write a story about a
horrid child. Horrid Henry was born on
the spot. I also wanted to write about sibling
rivalry and families where one child was
considered 'perfect' and the other 'horrid'.

Is Horrid Henry based on a real child?

No, but I think there's a bit of Henry and
Peter inside everyone.

Where do you get your ideas from?

I get my ideas from things that happen to me, or people I know, or from my imagination. I think of ordinary situations, like birthday parties or getting nits, then add a 'horrid' twist. So, if my son has to have an injection, I think of how Henry would behave.

Will there be any more Horrid Henry books?

Yes! *Horrid Henry and the Mega-Mean Time Machine* will be published in 2005 and *Horrid Henry and the Abominable Snowman* in 2006.

How long does it take to write a Horrid Henry book?

Around four months.

Who is your favourite character?

I like Moody Margaret, because I was bossy like her when I was her age. But of

course, I love Henry and Peter. And Beefy
Bert makes me laugh.

What's your favourite Horrid Henry story?

I usually like the one I'm writing at the
moment best, but old favourites
include *Horrid Henry Gets Rich
Quick* and *Horrid
Henry's Injection*. I'm
scared of
injections and
it makes me
laugh when
I read it.

Will Horrid Henry be on TV?

Yes! A cartoon series is being created this minute.

Do you like writing books?

YES! But I hate starting a new book. I am happiest when I am improving my rough drafts.

How do you get your characters' names?

I think of funny adjectives, like 'sour' or 'rude', and match names to them. I love alliteration and use it as much as possible.

Who is you favourite writer?

My favourite author as a child was Edward Eager, who wrote about magic adventures. I also really liked Beverly Cleary, whose Ramona and Henry Huggins books are published here. My favourite author now is Anthony Trollope, a Victorian novelist who wrote forty-three very long books.

How many books have you written?

I've written over forty books.

What was your first book called?

What Does the Hippopotamus Say?

What's your favourite book that you've written?

Helping Hercules, about a girl who finds a magic coin and goes back to ancient Greece to sort out the Greek heroes.

Where do you write?

On a computer in my very messy office in the attic of my Victorian house.

Why did you want to be an author?

I've always enjoyed writing, and started writing fairy tales when I was eight years old, so it is never too early to start. I used to be a journalist, but I became an author after my son Joshua was born in 1989. I started writing because I kept getting ideas – I think it's because I love reading, and I was reading a lot of children's books then. It did take me over a year to have my first book accepted, though.

Can you give me any writing tips?

Ideas are everywhere, and you must listen out for them. Your stories will be more fun if you give them a twist. So, if you want to write about football, what about an alien football match, or a pets' football match? It's always easier to write the beginning and end first and the middle last. Think of where your character is at the beginning, and what they are like, and how they are different at the end. The middle bit is what changed them. The best way to learn to be a writer is to be a reader.

Do any famous footballers like your books?

I don't know, but maybe one day we'll spot Michael Owen sitting with a *Horrid Henry* book between goals!

Happy reading!

Francesca Simon

The HORRID HENRY books
By Francesca Simon
Illustrated by Tony Ross

Horrid Henry
Horrid Henry and the Secret Club
Horrid Henry Tricks the Tooth Fairy
Horrid Henry's Nits
Horrid Henry Gets Rich Quick
Horrid Henry's Haunted House
Horrid Henry and the Mummy's Curse
Horrid Henry's Revenge
Horrid Henry and the Bogey Babysitter
Horrid Henry's Stinkbomb
Horrid Henry's Underpants
Horrid Henry Meets the Queen
Horrid Henry's Joke Book
Horrid Henry's Big Bad Book
Ten favourite stories about Horrid Henry
at school, with lots of extra bits and illus-
trations in colour!

And coming shortly –
Horrid Henry and the Mega-Mean Time
Machine

The **HORRID HENRY** books are also
available on audio cassette and CD,
all read by Miranda Richardson

If you like Francesca Simon's
writing, and Tony Ross's illustrations,
you will also enjoy

HELPING HERCULES

A fabulously funny story in which the Greek
myths are told as they've never been told
before!

and coming shortly

Don't Cook Cinderella

A school story with a difference! Miss Bad
Fairy is inciting her pupils the Big Bad Wolf,
Troll and the wicked stepmother to gobble up
Miss Good Fairy's class. What will the three
little pigs, Cinderella and Snow White do? A
hilarious and thoroughly subversive new twist
on favourite fairy tale characters.